For Geraldine, Joe, Naomi, Eddie, Laura and Isaac
M.R.

For Elaine, Charlotte and Nicola
A.R.

SIMON AND SCHUSTER BOOKS FOR YOUNG READERS
Simon & Schuster Building, Rockefeller Center
1230 Avenue of the Americas, New York, New York 10020

Text Copyright © 1990 by Michael Rosen
Illustrations Copyright © 1990 by Arthur Robins
All rights reserved including the right of reproduction
in whole or in part in any form.

Originally published in Great Britain by Walker Books Limited
First U.S. edition 1990
SIMON AND SCHUSTER BOOKS FOR YOUNG READERS
is a trademark of Simon & Schuster Inc.

Manufactured in Italy

10 9 8 7 6 5 4 3 2 1

Library of Congress Cataloging-in-Publication Data
Rosen, Michael, Little Rabbit Foo Foo.

Summary: Naughty Rabbit Foo Foo, who mistreats the
other forest inhabitants, receives his just deserts from the
Good Fairy. [1. Rabbits—Fiction. 2. Behavior—Fiction]
I. Robins, Arthur, ill. II. Title. PZ7.R71867Li 1990 [E]
90-9598 ISBN 0-671-70968-2

Little Rabbit Foo Foo

Retold by Michael Rosen
Illustrated by Arthur Robins

SIMON AND SCHUSTER BOOKS FOR YOUNG READERS

Published by Simon & Schuster Inc., New York

Little Rabbit Foo Foo

riding through the forest,

scooping up the field mice

and bopping them on the head.

Down came the Good Fairy and
she said, "Little Rabbit Foo Foo,
I don't like your attitude,
scooping up the field mice
and bopping them on the head.
I'm going to give you three
chances to change, and if you
don't, I'm going to turn you
into a goon."

Little Rabbit Foo Foo
riding through the forest,

scooping up the wriggly worms
and bopping them on the head.

Down came the Good Fairy

and she said, "Little Rabbit Foo Foo,
I don't like your attitude,
scooping up the wriggly worms
and bopping them on the head.
You've got two chances to change,
and if you don't, I'm going to
turn you into a goon."

Little Rabbit Foo Foo
riding through the forest,
scooping up the tigers
and bopping them on the head.

Down came the Good Fairy and
she said, "Little Rabbit Foo Foo,
I don't like your attitude,
scooping up the tigers
and bopping them on the head.

"You've got one chance left to change,
and if you don't, I'm going to
turn you into a goon."

Little Rabbit Foo Foo
riding through the forest,
scooping up the goblins

and bopping them on the head.

Down came the Good Fairy and
she said, "Little Rabbit Foo Foo,
I don't like your attitude,
scooping up the goblins
and bopping them on the head.

"You've got no chances left, so I'm
going to turn you into a goon."

And she did.